THE GOOD-GUY CAKE

Barbara Dillon

illustrated by Alan Tiegreen

William Morrow and Company
New York   1980

Printed in the United States of America.
1 2 3 4 5 6 7 8 9 10

Library of Congress Cataloging in Publication Data

Dillon, Barbara.
  The good-guy cake.
  Summary: When Martin eats a magic cake that makes him anxious to behave perfectly and please everyone, he finds that his new behavior has some drawbacks.
  [1. Behavior—Fiction] I. Tiegreen, Alan. II. Title.
PZ7.D57916Go [Fic] 80-14514
ISBN 0-688-22240-4
ISBN 0-688-32240-9 (lib. bdg.)

To my mother and father

"**M**artin Bennett, get out of my closet this instant!" yelled Martin's sister, Mary. "What are you doing in this room anyway?" 2104349

"I'm looking for my ball," explained Martin, backing hastily toward the door.

"Well, it's not in here," Mary said. She looked at her brother more closely. "What have you got all over your mouth?" she demanded.

"Nothing," said Martin, nervously putting his sticky hands behind his back.

"It's chocolate!" Mary screamed.

"You found that Mars Bar in my sewing box. You stole my candy!"

Martin didn't stop to answer. He turned and ran.

"If I ever find you in here again, I'll kill you!" Mary shouted after him.

Martin bounded downstairs just as fast as his legs could carry him.

"Martin, look what you're doing to my new wallpaper!" cried his mother. She was standing in the hallway glaring up at him. Martin glanced in alarm at the wall next to him. It was covered with chocolatey finger marks.

Oh-oh, I'm in trouble, he thought.

"How many times have I told you to keep your hands off the wall and use the banister?" his mother wailed.

"That's what it's there for."

"I'm sorry," said Martin. "I'll remember next time."

He particularly wanted his mother to be in a good mood today, because he had something very important to ask her, something he and his best friend, Charlie Miles, had just finished talking about on the telephone. As a matter of fact, he had been on his way downstairs to find her when he had been sidetracked by the interesting possibilities of Mary's empty room. Now he would have to wait awhile until his mother cooled off.

Martin went into the living room and snapped on the television. He snapped it off again, did a somersault, got down on his hands and knees to look for a quarter that he had lost under the couch the week before, and then, figuring he had given his mother enough time to recover, headed doggedly for the kitchen.

Mrs. Bennett was busy swabbing the floor with her sponge mop.

"Don't come in," she said sharply. "The floor is all wet."

"Can-I-go-to-the-school-fair-next-week-on-my-bike-Charlie-Miles'-mom-is-letting-him-and-I-would-be-very-careful-and-ride-over-to-the-side-of-the-road-so-I-don't-get-killed." Martin took a deep breath and looked eagerly at his mother.

"You would have to go along the

Post Road to get to the school," Mrs. Bennett said, without looking up from her mopping. "There would be too much traffic. I would worry the whole time you were gone."

"Charlie Miles' mom isn't going to worry," said Martin. "And I'm a better rider than Charlie is."

"Well, I can't help it. I would worry," said his mother, squeezing out the mop into the bucket at her side.

"I would go really slowly and not try anything crazy," Martin promised.

"No," said his mother firmly. "Dad or I will drive you over to the fair. But you may not ride your bike."

"How come Brad gets to take his bike, and I don't?" Martin asked, his voice trembling with indignation. But he already knew what his mother's answer would be.

"Your brother is almost three years older than you," she said. "Next spring you'll be able to ride your bike to the fair for sure."

"Next spring!" shouted Martin. "That's a whole year away! I don't know how you can be so mean!"

"I love you, Marty. And I don't want you to get hurt," said his mother.

"You don't love me. You only love Brad, and that's why he always gets to do stuff and I don't," said Martin hotly. He knew this wasn't true, but sometimes he wanted to think that it was. His mother started to say something else, but Martin clapped his hands to his ears so he wouldn't have to hear whatever dumb, mothery thing it was sure to be and ran from the kitchen.

"She is so mean," he said to himself, as he stamped down the hall. And to spite her, he kicked the door of the den as he entered, deliberately trying to leave a scuff mark on it.

At the desk by the window his big brother, Brad, was working on his stamp collection. Martin would have liked to collect stamps too. But of course his parents said no, not until he was older and more responsible.

Martin stood in the doorway for a moment and then moved over to the desk to get a better look at the red-

and-yellow stamp Brad was examining through a magnifying glass. Spread out around him were a lot of other stamps, all brightly colored and fascinating.

"Look out, Marty, you're standing in my light," said Brad.

Martin frowned. "I can stand here if I want to," he said. "This den belongs to me too."

"Move, Dumbhead," said Brad, giving Martin an absentminded shove with his free hand. Martin did not shove back. He just leaned over Brad's shoulder and blew as hard as he could, sending a cloud of stamps swirling in all directions.

"Okay, you asked for it," said Brad, jumping to his feet.

"I'm sorry, I'm sorry," yelped
Martin, flying out of the den with Brad
at his heels. Down the hall the two
boys ran and into the kitchen, narrowly missing their mother's water
bucket.

"Can't you see I'm doing the floor?"
she cried, as Martin and Brad fled past
her. They raced through the kitchen

door and into the backyard where their father was raking the lawn.

"Brad's going to punch me," gasped Martin, running to his father.

"Martin blew my stamps all over the den. He deserves to be punched," shouted Brad, trying to get at Martin, who was using Mr. Bennett as a shield.

"All right, all right," said Mr. Bennett, fending Brad off with one arm. "No punching or stamp blowing allowed on Saturdays between 9:35 and 11:02 A.M. Martin, you stay out here with me. Brad, you go back inside."

"Okay, but next time I'm really going to get him," muttered Brad threateningly.

Waiting till his brother was safely

back inside, Martin turned to his father. "Dad, can I ride my bike to the Ferguson Frolics next Saturday?"

"Have you spoken to your mother about it?" inquired Mr. Bennett.

"She says there would be too much traffic," Martin said scornfully. "I'm a good bike rider, Dad. I could do it easily."

Mr. Bennett hesitated. For a moment he looked as if he were ready to say Yes. But then he seemed to think better of it.

"It's up to your mother," he said. "She knows best about these things. Now do you suppose you could just keep your eye on your little brother here for about five minutes while I finish getting the lawn in shape?" Mr. Bennett sighed and looked about him. "I don't believe how much there is to do around this place in the spring," he said. "And I still haven't found time to clean out the cellar."

Martin was disappointed all over again by his father's decision to leave the bike business up to his mother. He scowled at Tyler, his little brother, who was sitting on the ground taking pebbles out of one pocket and putting them into the other. Tyler looked at Martin and grinned, and drool rolled down his chin.

"What a sloppy baby," said Martin in disgust.

"He drools because he's getting a

new tooth," explained Mr. Bennett proudly.

"Everybody thinks it's so great every time Tyler gets a tooth," grumbled Martin. "He's not the only person in the world with teeth."

Tyler got to his feet and toddled over to Martin. He handed him one of his pebbles.

"I don't want that dumb thing," said Martin, giving Tyler a little push. Tyler staggered backward and sat down on the ground. He looked surprised. He gave Martin a big grin and got back up on his feet.

I guess he likes to be pushed, thought Martin, and he gave him another shove. This time Tyler sat

down much harder. This time he didn't grin. His lower lip curled out, and he began to howl. Martin's father turned from his raking just in time to see Tyler hit the ground.

"This is very disappointing behavior, Martin," he said, stooping to pick up a tearful Tyler in his arms. "Only last night I was remarking to Mom how you seemed to be really shaping up. You don't dawdle nearly so much, and you've been getting along a lot better with Brad. But now in the last ten minutes, you've blown his stamps all over the den and knocked down your younger brother. I want you in the house immediately—and stay away from Brad."

Martin walked sulkily toward the kitchen door, scuffing his new sneakers in the soft spring earth. It would serve all of them right if he ran away. Then they would have no one to yell at and pick on all the time. Then his mother would really have something to worry about, and he wouldn't even care or send her a postcard or anything.

"Hi, Martin. Want some cake?" Standing at the bottom of the driveway was Martin's neighbor, Myra McGarry. She had moved in across the street just a few weeks before, and Martin thought she was the weirdest girl he had ever met. Often he would see her running across the lawn with her arms outstretched, pretending to fly. Sometimes she wore a cape when she ran, and sometimes she wore a big pair of blue, plastic butterfly wings strapped around her shoulders.

"Someday I'm really gonna take off," she would tell him. "You just wait and see."

She also had a wand painted a dazzling orange. She was always going around tapping things with it, saying, "I turn you into a gerbil" or "a pirate" or "a midget." What was worse, she kept trying to get Martin to play these stupid games with her. He would certainly have ignored her now if she hadn't mentioned cake.

"Come on," she urged, grinning up at him. Martin took a quick look at his father, who was busy wiping Tyler's chin. Then he stole quietly down the driveway to where Myra stood waiting for him.

"Where is the cake?" he demanded.

"At my house," she said. "Let's go."

She better not be playing a trick on

me, Martin thought to himself, as he followed her reluctantly across the street. He hated tricks.

On the screened porch at the side of the McGarry house Myra had set out a small, white metal oven. Painted across the front in red letters were the words, *Little Homemaker's Magic Microwave.* Next to the oven was a mixing bowl, a wooden spoon, a couple of little boxes of cake mix, several cake pans, a measuring cup filled with water, and some pink paper napkins.

"My yittle oven really *is* magic, too," said Myra proudly. That was another awful thing about Myra. She said *yittle* when she meant *little.*

"Magic, my foot," scoffed Martin.

"They always call kids' stuff magic. That's just so kids will buy it. Don't you even know that?"

"Yes, I know that," Myra said. "Only this time I got a thing that does work. You just wait and see."

Carefully she unwound a black cord from the back of the oven and plugged it into a socket in the porch wall. At once a little red light flashed on at the top of the oven.

"Some magic," sneered Martin. But he sat down on the floor to get a closer look. Myra sat down next to him. From one of the boxes of mix she poured some sweet-smelling white flour into the mixing bowl. From the measuring cup she poured some water. With the

wooden spoon she began to stir the
batter slowly.

"What kind of cake is it going to
be?" asked Martin.

"Good-guy cake," said Myra.

"I've never heard of that kind," said
Martin.

"I know," said Myra. "That's why
you need some."

Martin looked at the cake pans.
"Use the biggest one," he ordered.

"You might be sorry if I do," warned
Myra.

"I won't get sick. Nothing makes me
sick," Martin boasted.

"Good-guy cake never makes *you*
sick," said Myra. "But sometimes it
makes other people sick."

"I don't know what you're talking about," said Martin. "Use the big pan."

"Well, okay," agreed Myra. "But don't blame me if anything goes wrong." She poured the batter into the largest pan and put it carefully into the oven.

"How long does it have to cook?" asked Martin.

"When the yittle red light goes off, the cake will be finished," Myra explained.

They both sat quietly watching the light. To pass the time, they played I Packed My Trunk, till Martin told Myra she was cheating. He also told her she had too many freckles on her nose.

"You really need a hunk of good-guy cake," Myra said. "You won't be such a pain after you have some."

At that moment the red light on the oven flashed off.

"It's ready," said Martin eagerly.

Myra opened the oven door, and a lovely, sweet cake smell floated out. She unfolded one of the paper napkins and turned the cake pan upside down over it. Neatly the little golden cake dropped into the napkin. Myra covered it with a second napkin, flipped it right side up, and handed it to Martin with a sly smile. "Now the fun begins," she said.

Martin wasted no time. He opened his mouth wide and took a big bite.

The cake was soft and sweet and light
as a feather. "Oh, yum. This is really
delicious," he said, taking another
huge bite.

"Doesn't my yittle oven make nice
cake?" Myra asked proudly.

"It sure does!" Martin sighed, as he
swallowed the last morsel. He licked
his sticky fingers and looked at Myra.

All at once he felt sorry he had told her she had too many freckles.

"Would you like me to stay and play with you?" he inquired politely. As the question slipped from his lips, he blinked in surprise. He certainly had not meant to ask her to play; no one in his right mind would want to do that. Myra grinned at him in a mocking sort of way that usually would have infuriated him, but now it didn't make him the least bit angry. All he felt was a sudden great need to be pleasant and obliging—to be a good guy.

So he and Myra played house all morning. Martin was the daddy and wore an old hat that had belonged to Myra's father. He wheeled Myra's dolls

up and down the driveway in an ex-
press wagon while Myra went flapping
past in her cape, tapping them with
her wand. Martin didn't object at all,
not even when she gave him a good
rap on the head and announced she
had just turned him into a ballerina.

When the time came to go home, he

thanked her for a nice morning and insisted upon helping her carry the dolls back to the porch. Myra was smiling her sly smile when Martin looked back at her as he rounded the corner of the house.

At lunch Martin amazed his mother by setting out the sandwiches and pouring everybody's milk. He lifted Tyler into his high chair and tied the bib around his neck. He even put the water on for his father's coffee. And all the while that strange feeling of wanting to be good, of wanting to be perfect, washed over him like a big splash of warm bath water.

"Why is Martin acting so weird?" Mary asked.

"What is so weird about helping your mother?" Mrs. Bennett demanded. "You should be so weird, Mary."

"Mary, your elbows are on the table," Martin whispered softly to his sister.

"What business is it of yours?" hissed Mary.

"Golly, Brad, I think you forgot to wash your hands," said Martin to his brother. "They look pretty grubby to me."

"Will somebody please strangle him?" asked Brad, glaring at Martin.

"I would like to eat my egg-salad sandwich in peace. Is that too much to ask?" said Mr. Bennett.

"It sure isn't, Dad," said Martin. "Here, have another," and he passed the plate of sandwiches to his father, who looked surprised and pleased and then looked at Mrs. Bennett to see what she made of it.

"What's he up to anyway?" muttered Brad suspiciously. "He's really being strange."

"There was nothing strange about him this morning when he stole the candy out of my closet," said Mary with a shrug. "He was the same old Martin then."

"Sorry about that candy, Mary," said Martin. "I don't know what got into me. I'll get you some more. I promise."

And that is just what he did. As

soon as lunch was finished, he took
money from his piggy bank and ran
down to the corner store. He bought
Mary a Mars Bar, and he bought a box
of raisins for himself.

"Fruit is much better for you than
sweets," he told the clerk behind the
counter, and he ran out of the store,
leaving the astonished clerk staring
after him.

At home, Martin went straight to
his room and got out crayons and
construction paper. Briskly he set to
work making a sign. The sign read:
For a super sister. He drew several
spaceships around the edge of the paper
and laid the sign along with the chocolate bar on Mary's desk. As he was

turning to leave, Mary suddenly ap-
peared in the doorway.

"Look, Mary, see what I brought
you," he said, pointing hastily to the
candy bar.

"Gee, Marty, that's really nice of
you," said Mary, staring at it in wonder.
She looked admiringly at the spaceships
on Martin's poster.

34

"I'm going to be an astronaut when I grow up," she remarked, tacking the poster to the bulletin board above her desk. She broke the candy bar in two and handed one half to Martin. "Girls can do anything boys can do," she told him sternly. 2104349

Martin started to say "Oh, yeah?" and name several things he was sure girls couldn't do, but on this strange day, when all he wanted was to please everyone, he heard himself agreeing with her, even though in his heart he was sure she was wrong.

He finished his candy and walked to the door, pausing for a moment to look at his sister. "You know something," he said, "being good is fun."

"Not always," said Mary. "Last week I was the best I've ever been. I saved my allowance when I wanted to spend it. I kept my room super neat, which is a pain. I handed in every homework assignment on time. It was no fun at all, and no one even said 'Good job, Mary.'"

Martin thought about what she had said as he went downstairs. Maybe being good was a lot harder than it seemed.

"Hey, Marty, can I borrow your handcuffs?" Brad asked, as Martin walked into the kitchen. "I'm going over to Scott Savage's, and I'd like to have them so we can practice locking each other up."

Martin sighed. Brad was always getting yelled at for losing things. Besides, the handcuffs were practically brand-new.

"Okay, if you promise not to lose them," he agreed reluctantly. And then all at once, swept by a sudden, surprising wave of generosity, he said, "You can keep them if you want, Brad."

"Oh, wow, that's great," said Brad, running out of the kitchen. "Thanks a lot, Marty."

Martin sat down at his mother's desk and began doodling on a note pad.

"Now I would like to do something nice for Mom and Dad," he said to himself. "But what?" He thought

about buying them a present, but he
had only thirty-seven cents left in his
bank. He thought about making them
a picture, but the refrigerator was
already covered with his artwork. Suddenly he had a brainstorm. He would
clean out the cellar. That was something that would please them both. He
jumped to his feet and rushed to the
cellar door. Even the steps down which
he bounded had things piled on them.

It's going to be an awful big job, he
thought, looking around the untidy
basement. I'd better get started right
away. And then he had a second
tremendous idea.

I'll have a tag sale out on the lawn,
he decided. That way I can make some

money and please my family at the same time. I can please the neighbors too. I may end up pleasing practically the whole town!

The house was very quiet as Martin set eagerly to work. Tyler and his mother were napping. His father had gone into town, and Brad and Mary had both gone out.

The first thing Martin brought up from the basement was a red-and-yellow cardboard lemonade stand. It had a wide counter and a shelf underneath on which he could pile things. He was sorry the stand had *Lemonade 3¢ a Glass* printed on it, but at least its bright colors would attract customers, he thought. As he wiped dust from the counter with his sleeve, he looked approvingly at all the cars passing by. His mother was always saying how she wished they didn't live on such a busy street, but for that very reason Mary used to be able to sell gallons of watery lemonade on hot summer days.

Back and forth Martin trudged, lugging up from the cellar magazines and cans of paint and odd bits of furniture and a large carton of old toys. He was just emerging from the kitchen with an empty mayonnaise jar in which to put his money when his first customers, a boy and girl, arrived.

"We would like these double runners for our little brother," the boy said. "How much are they?"

40

"Fifty cents," Martin told him, suddenly wondering as he took the boy's money if perhaps he should have saved the skates for Tyler. "Oh, well," he told himself, "with all the money I'll make I can buy Tyler a new pair."

A woman and her husband came by next. They bought a bridge lamp and a can of white paint and five 1966 issues of a magazine called *Fly Fishing Digest.*

"How much are you asking for these mason jars, son?" a man wearing tennis shorts inquired. "My wife could use them for her corn relish."

"Dad, will you buy me this neat stuffed rabbit?" his little girl asked. Martin was becoming quite muddled making change. But he was happy about the growing pile of nickels and dimes and quarters.

Myra came by and bought a doll-size rolling pin of Mary's.

"Now I can bake some yittle pies," she said, handing Martin his money.

"What in the world is going on here?" asked Mr. Bennett, suddenly appearing at Martin's elbow. "Why are all these people milling around on my lawn?"

"I'm having a tag sale, Dad," Martin said proudly. "Want to buy something?"

"How much is this wildcat suit?" asked a boy, stepping in front of Mr. Bennett.

"That's not for sale, I'm afraid," said Mr. Bennett quickly, plucking the suit

from the boy's hands. He turned to
Martin with a reproachful look.

"How did my high-school cheerlead-
ing costume get in the toy box?" he
demanded. "I'd be very upset if anything happened to it."

At the same moment, Brad came up
the driveway, and Mrs. Bennett, carry-

ing Tyler, stepped out of the house.

"I thought I heard thumping and bumping on the stairs," she said, looking around in surprise. "But I had no idea anything like this was going on."

"Why is my Chutes and Ladders game out here?" demanded Brad. "I hope you weren't trying to sell it, Marty."

All at once Mrs. Bennett gave a squeal. "What happened to my mason jars!" she cried. "I'm planning to pickle my cucumbers this summer."

"But I didn't think anybody wanted any of this stuff!" said Martin, tears springing to his eyes. "I was trying to make some money so I could buy all you guys presents."

"Want pwesent," said Tyler.

Mrs. Bennett looked at Martin, with a mixture of exasperation and tenderness. "It was a very nice thought, Marty," she said. "It's just that you should have asked permission first."

Mr. Bennett, smiling, caught Martin's head in the crook of his arm and gave it an affectionate squeeze. "No real harm done, Marty," he said. "Actually, a tag sale is a good idea. Maybe the whole family can organize one in a few weeks when we've had a chance to clear out more junk around this place. But in the meantime, how about you and Brad tackling the cellar together tomorrow morning? I'll pay you four bucks apiece. But if I hear any arguing or fighting, the deal is off."

"Okay, Dad," agreed Martin, his spirits soaring again immediately.

"If we do a really terrific job, will you give us a tip?" asked Brad.

"We'll see," said Mr. Bennett. "Now let's all help Martin move this stuff back into the house before any more customers come. We can sort through it tomorrow and see what we want to save."

Everyone gathered up something. Even Tyler tried to help by picking up a paintbrush, which he immediately crammed in his mouth.

In the excitement of his tag sale Martin had forgotten for a while about the Ferguson Frolics. But now as he

plodded up the cellar stairs to the kitchen he remembered how disappointed he was to have to be driven there like a baby.

Tyler greeted him with a big smile. "Cookie," he said, holding out a soggy bit of brownie.

Martin looked at it sorrowfully. "I would rather ride my bike to the fair next week than have a chocolate brownie today," he said, hoping his mother was noticing how sad he was.

She noticed. "Marty," she said, shaking her head, "You're acting like an absolute dingbat about this bike thing." Thoughtfully she felt his forehead. "You look flushed," she told him. "Are you sure you feel okay?"

"I'm fine, Mother," said Martin with a forlorn smile.

Mrs. Bennett put her hands firmly on his shoulders and headed him toward the door. "I think you should go watch the ball game with Dad," she said. "Maybe it will help you to relax a little. You've been so keyed up ever since lunch."

"Okay," Martin said obligingly. He gave Tyler an absentminded pat on the head and trotted out of the kitchen and down the hall, being careful to keep his hands off the new wallpaper.

In the den his father and Brad and Mary, who had come home from her friend's, were all glued to the television set.

"A homer!" they cried together, as Martin sat down on the couch.

"That son of a gun must have driven the ball four hundred feet," exclaimed Mr. Bennett excitedly.

"What son of a gun?" asked Martin.

"Mickey Rivers," said Brad, and he jumped up from his chair and began dancing around the room, hitting imaginary line drives with an imaginary bat.

Martin began to fidget as the urge to do another good deed stirred within him once again.

"Brad and I could start on the cellar now, before supper," he offered.

"I'm not starting now," said Brad indignantly. "Can't you see I'm watch-

ing the ball game? Honest, Marty, you have been the biggest nerd today."

Martin was stung by his brother's words, especially as his mother had just said he was acting like a dingbat.

"Am I a nerd, Mary?" he asked his sister anxiously.

"Well, sort of, Marty," she said.

"Am I, Dad?" Martin asked Mr. Bennett.

"No, I wouldn't say a nerd exactly," said his father. But he sounded rather uncertain.

Martin sighed deeply and scratched his head. He had so wanted to please them all. But he seemed to be doing just the opposite. Well, if they all preferred the old Martin Bennett, then that is what he would have to give them—that is, if he still could.

Martin rose slowly from the couch and walked slowly from the den and not quite so slowly out the front door, and then he raced down the driveway and across the street to Myra's house.

He found her sitting on the porch
with a pack of fortune-telling cards
spread out in front of her.

"Myra," he said breathlessly. "You
were right about the good-guy cake.
You told me if I ate too much it might
make other people sick, and that's just
what's happened. I've been so good all

day my family can't take it anymore. Do you have any cake that can make me a little bit bad again?"

"Sure," said Myra calmly. "My yittle oven can bake anything." She pushed aside the cards and plugged in the oven once more. This time she poured into the mixing bowl a dark-brown, spicy-smelling flour from the other box of cake mix.

"Can I stir?" asked Martin, as she carefully added the water.

But Myra shook her head. "I'm the one who has to make this yittle cake," she told him.

"It looks like a mudpie," said Martin.

"This is no mudpie," Myra told him

solemnly. Her spoon went round and round in the batter till it was smooth and shiny.

"We can finish playing I Packed My Trunk while it bakes," she said, pouring the batter into a tiny cake pan no bigger than a thimble. But the cake, because of its small size, was done before she and Martin had even reached the letter *F*.

Martin popped the whole thing into his mouth at once. The flavor this time was ginger, and although it was not as sweet as good-guy cake, it was just as delicious.

"Marty, time for supper!" Martin heard his mother call. Slowly he ran the tip of his tongue over his lips to be sure he had got the last spicy crumb.

"I wish there were more," he said.

"Prob'ly you've had enough," said Myra wisely.

"Prob'ly you're right," agreed Martin. "So long, Myra, and thanks." And he turned and tore across her backyard toward home. As he ran, he leaped up to touch the branches of each tree he passed, and in his own driveway he hopped over a big plastic truck of Tyler's and for good measure turned around and hopped over it twice more. The strange, anxious desire to behave perfectly and to please everybody all the time had vanished. He felt fine. He felt like a dog who had rolled in the dirt after a bath and

got back his own good familiar smell again.

"Martin, I don't like your disappearing just before mealtime," said Mrs. Bennett, as Martin came rushing into the dining room.

"I had some important business to take care of," he explained, flopping into his chair. "How come Brad is hogging all the French fries?"

"There are plenty of potatoes for everyone," Mr. Bennett assured him.

"Mom, Martin called me a hog!" said Brad.

"At least he's acting normal again," said Mary.

"Everyone eat before the dinner gets cold," commanded Mrs. Bennett.

Mr. Bennett took a forkful of salad and looked consideringly at Martin.

"Marty, Mom and I were having a chat just before dinner," he said. "And we decided the reason you have been trying so hard to be good all day is to let us know that you are ready to handle a little responsibility. We think you've done a pretty good job, so we've decided to let you ride your bike to the fair."

"Even though I still wish you'd let Dad drive you," Mrs. Bennett added with a worried smile.

"Yippee!" cried Martin, his elbow narrowly missing Brad's milk glass as he lifted his arms in a triumphant cheer.

60

"Go fair," said Tyler from his high
chair.

"Tyler too little," said Martin in a
kindly voice. "I'll bring you a balloon
though, a nice red one."

For once his parents had treated
him like a grown-up. Martin felt just
about ready for anything. But he
couldn't help wondering what his
mother and father would say if he told
them about Myra's oven.

They would think that it was only

the cake that was making me good, and then they would change their minds about letting me ride my bike, he decided. He bit thoughtfully into the chicken leg on his plate.

"But it wasn't just the cake," he said to himself. "Being good makes you feel good inside, which makes you want to go on being good forever. The thing is, though, no one can be good *all* the time. Besides, people don't even like it if you are. They think you're some kind of big phoney and they end up saying, 'That guy really makes me sick,' which is just what Myra said would happen."

Martin chased some peas around his plate with the fork. His thoughts drifted to the rolling pin Myra had bought at his tag sale. He wondered what kind of pie she was planning to bake in that looney oven of hers.

"Well, no way will she get me to have a slice, no way," he told himself. "Unless," and he paused with his fork raised in midair, "the name of her pie is something really special like smart-guy pie. Then maybe I might try just a teeny piece."

Dreamily he wiped his mouth with his napkin. Already he could imagine himself turning into the smartest boy in his class. He would be so smart they would keep promoting him till he caught up with Brad and then with Mary and finally ended up in college

before he was nine years old. They
would put him on television, and he
would win many valuable prizes—
basketballs and ten-speed bikes and
trips to Disney World. He began to
feel very excited. He looked expec-
tantly around the table at his family.
Maybe by this time tomorrow night,
depending of course on Myra and her
oven, he would have a big surprise for
them all. Maybe, just maybe, they
would find themselves dining with a
brand-new Martin Bennett—a Martin
Bennett who would astound them—a
Martin Bennett who would absolutely,
positively bowl them over.